This book belongs to

....

For Phoebe and Willow who keep me smiling.

Thank you to my beta readers for their amazing input and kind words and to Pam whose hard work helped to make this the book that it is.

Finally, thank you to Toni who continues to support everything that I do with endless patience and love and without whom none of this would be possible.

MONSTACADEMY
THE HALLOWEEN PARADE

Printed in the United Kingdom
First Printing, 2017

A CIP catalogue record for this book is available from the British Library.

ISBN (Standard Edition): 978-1-9997244-2-9
ISBN (Dyslexia Friendly): 978-1-9997244-3-6
Also available as an eBook

www.mattbeighton.co.uk
www.greenmonkeypress.co.uk

MONSTACADEMY

The Halloween Parade

CHAPTER 1

The Letter

To most children, their school seems perfectly ordinary. I imagine that yours is the same. I bet that when you turned up for school this morning there was little chance of you bumping into a Werewolf. There are probably not many Vampires in your class. The chance of you sitting next to a Ghost or Banshee in maths is, I would guess, very remote.

This was also true of St. Agatha's Primary School. St Agatha's was a lovely, small school with a tree-lined playing field and with just enough children to keep it interesting but not quite enough to be big and scary. Trixie Grimble, our heroine, is nine and three quarters. Until recently, St Agatha's had been her school.

It had all started with a letter, as these things so

often do. This particular letter had arrived at the beginning of July in a neat brown envelope with a lovely, handwritten address on the front and was stamped with the mark of Wexbridge Borough Council. It was plainly labelled for the attention of Trixie Grimble. However, Trixie's mum, upon finding the letter lying there on the doormat, had done what mothers so often do when they think that they know best. She had opened it herself.

Dear Miss Grimble,

We are so sorry to inform you that due to budget cuts at Wexbridge Borough Council we are closing St. Agatha's Primary School.

However, please do not panic. We have been able to find you a place at Monroe's Academy for the Different. We do hope that you enjoy your time there. They are very much looking forward to welcoming you into their halls.

Yours sincerely

Mr Bothwold-Oxelton

Mr Bothwold-Oxelton

P.S. In order to make up for this terrible inconvenience, I have enclosed a coupon for a year's supply of toilet paper from Keith's Toilet Emporium on the High Street.

Well, you can imagine the scream that Mrs Grimble let out upon reading the letter. It quite disturbed Mrs Burbage, the nosey next-door neighbour who was stood near to the open kitchen window listening for titbits of information whilst pretending to trim her bush.

Trixie had been peacefully sleeping in her bedroom when her mum's shriek had echoed through the house and rudely woken her from a lovely dream. Leaping from her bed and racing down the stairs, nearly tripping over her ancient and overweight pet cat, Snot, in the process, Trixie found her mum in quite the tizz.

"What is it, Mum?" she asked sleepily. "Is that a letter? It's addressed to me!" she shouted, suddenly awake and noticing the open and now empty brown envelope slowly soaking in a bowl of cereal where her mum had dropped it. It had been torn neatly along the top edge. Trixie snatched the note from her mum's unresisting hand and read it for herself.

"Monroe's Academy for the Different?" Trixie

gasped, not believing the evidence in front of her very nose. "I can't go there, and you can't make me! You do know what they call it, don't you? Monstacademy!" she continued, quite agitated because, quite rightly, nobody likes moving to a new school.

Trixie loved her mum in the way that all children do, and she was sure that her mum loved her back in her own way. They had never been very close preferring to go about their business on their own and occasionally meeting up for dinner in the kitchen. Trixie had long believed that her mother would prefer it if they both had separate houses to themselves and didn't get under each other's feet so often. Now, it seemed, she would get her wish.

Trixie had quite a nice group of friends at St Agatha's, and she didn't really think that she needed any new ones. Certainly none that went to Monstacademy! And what was worse was that Monroe's Academy for the Different was just that. It was a school for the different.

Now, when you or I think about people that

are different, we might think of somebody who is considerably shorter or very much taller than most or who might have a head full of vivid purple hair or perhaps who has a large boil on the end of their nose just waiting to be popped or maybe even somebody who looks a little bit like a potato.

That is not the type of different child that Monroe's Academy for the Different usually takes in. You see, Monstacademy was really very different indeed. Many of the pupils who attended were what you or I might call the supernatural.

Wait, I hear you asking, do you mean that there is a school for superheroes and those with special powers?

Were you to ask me that question I would simply scoff and say, "Of course not, that is ridiculous!" Instead, Monstacademy is a school for those of a spookier nature such as Vampires, Werewolves and even the odd Witch or Wizard.

Trixie was all too aware of the type of people that attended Monstacademy. There were always rumours at school about how their Vampire pupils would be sent down into the village for sucking practise or the Bogie-boys and -girls would be instructed to hide under the beds of normal boys and girls to practise making them scream with fear. She didn't like it one bit.

"You know as well as I do that I've wanted to get Trixie into a boarding school for a long time. I never meant somewhere like this, though! I had high hopes for Snufflingberrys or Blimpingtons. They'll drink her blood and turn her into a zombie! What will the neighbours think if she's off flying around all night as a bat?" her mother had sobbed to her boyfriend Rob when he'd returned home from work on that fateful day.

Trixie's dad had run away with his rock band when she was tiny and her mum's current boyfriend, Rob, had been living with them for a year now. Trixie didn't like him one bit. His company manufactured toothbrush bristles. Rob's job was to sell them to all sorts of companies in all sorts of exotic countries, and he often spent days away from home. He was also the sort of adult who thought he was really good at talking to children, but in fact he was boring and patronising and didn't actually like spending any time with them. He'd made this very clear when Trixie overheard him talking to her mum on the stairs one evening, a few days after the letter had arrived.

"Now listen," he'd began, reassuringly, "I'm going to be working away a lot for the next year, and you don't really want to be left alone to look after a growing girl, do you? Monstacademy is a boarding school. She'll be living there. You'll have all that time for yourself. You know how you've always wanted the time to train a cat circus? Well, now you'll have that time! Besides, she'll be much better off around other children. She'll get bored here just you two."

"Well, there is that. In a way it would be kinder to send her. But what about the other children? I've heard that they have Vampires and Zombies and everything else there. They might try to suck her blood!"

"Well, everyone needs a hobby, dear," he'd

replied, clearly unconcerned about Trixie's neck or the threat of eternal damnation. "Besides, those are just rumours. It's probably just a few extra hairy kids and some of those moody ones that like to wear black and listen to depressing music. You know the ones I mean…"

"Teenagers?" offered her mum.

"Yeah probably," Rob trailed off, distracted by a most terribly important business call on his mobile phone.

And that had been that. Rob had persuaded her mum that a little time to herself would be a good thing. In the end, even though she was never comfortable with Trixie mixing with what her mother had called "their sort", she'd decided that having her out of the house was worth the risk. She'd even spent time looking for kittens that looked suitably athletic. Trixie's displeasure had only been matched by Snot's who now spent most of his time on top of the fridge in protest.

"You'll make lots of new and exciting friends!" her mum had argued after one particularly bad fight.

"But, Mum," she'd wailed, "I am nearly ten years old, I'm pretty sure I've got all the friends I'll ever need!"

So it had continued throughout the summer. Eventually the holidays had drawn to an end, uniforms and equipment had been bought and Trixie soon found herself stood at the front door to her new life.

CHAPTER 2

Monstacademy

Trixie and her mum stood in the pouring rain at the bottom of the enormous, polished stone steps that led up to the giant wooden doors at the front of Monroe's Academy for the Different. The school stood at the top of a large hill that seemed to stand guard over the town of Wexbridge far below.

The large doors were the only entrance through the high brick walls that formed the courtyard that surrounded the school building. Tall towers rose up here and there that housed the classrooms and dormitories where the children would stay. The school could only be reached along a winding gravel road and looked a lot like the haunted castles that you see in comic books.

The school emblem was a brightly coloured

shield with the initials M.A.D written across it. At the bottom of the shield, a golden scroll was engraved with the school motto *"Nullum dolum, nullas agit animum advertamus!"* (No trick or treating!).

In case you were still unsure whether Monroe's Academy for the Different was a normal school, there was a large wooden sign that had been stuck to the wall next to the door. It read:

At Monroe's, we're all different!

In smaller letters that rather ruined the effect, somebody had scribbled:

Deliveries to the rear entrance please!

The other indication that this was a school for the extraordinary, if any more were needed, was the appearance of the pupils that moved in and out of the school as Trixie and her mum stood and watched.

Overhead, a girlishly giggling group of young Vampires chose that moment to fly over the top of the school walls and disappear into the courtyard beyond. Hanging out of one the upper-floor windows was a young boy with very long hair. He was screaming at the top of his lungs to a pair of equally long-haired boys who were pushing and shoving each other as they approached the school. Their long hair was damp and stuck to their bodies and a strong smell of wet dog filled the air as they stumbled up the steps and barged past Trixie and her mum.

"Oh, I am sorry," one of them grumbled. Each word sounded like the bark of a small dog. "Werewolf coming through!"

The boys both started laughing at what they clearly thought was a funny joke. Trixie didn't agree. A shiver ran down her spine that had nothing to do with the pouring rain that hammered down around them and that perfectly reflected her mood.

Her mum, on the other hand, seemed indifferent to the extraordinary characters that would soon become part of Trixie's everyday life. It could have been because Trixie was starting a new school and she wanted to show her that it would be all right, as mothers are so often keen to do.

More likely, Trixie suspected it had to do with being rid of her for a while. Her mum had brought home a litter of kittens the week before and was already trying to train them to sit and stand on two feet. All they had managed to do up until now, as far as Trixie could tell, was go to the toilet on the carpet and cry all night.

Despite the worsening weather, Trixie's mum looked positively cheerful and was busy bustling her towards the door whilst at the same time scraping a battered suitcase up the wide steps and trying to hold a flimsy umbrella over her head. She was trying her very best to get her reluctant daughter to do as she was told and come and meet the new teachers who she was quite sure would be just lovely.

It didn't take them long to reach the doors. Much sooner than Trixie would have liked, her mum was rapping the heavy iron knocker against the old wood. A tiny hatch that was cut into the door just above Trixie's head slid back and a small pair of eyes stared out at the two visitors. The eyes were bright yellow and bloodshot. Trixie and her mum took a step backwards so that the eyes could see them clearly.

"Hello?" came a put-upon voice from behind the doors that creaked and rasped like an old tree in a cemetery.

"Well, hello!" chirped Trixie's mum. "My name is Philomena Grimble. I have brought my lovely young daughter, Trixie, with me. She is due to start at your academy today." Trixie had never heard her mum speak in such a posh voice and she most certainly never referred to herself at Philomena. She was always Phillis to her friends. No doubt she was trying to make the best impression on the new school.

The voice on the other side of the door didn't reply, but the eyes disappeared and the hatch slammed shut. The sound of a large bolt being slid back was followed by the heavy wooden door swinging inwards and the owner of the yellow eyes stepping forwards to greet Trixie and her mum.

The eyes belonged to a very short, very unusual young man who looked like he had lost a wrestling match with a sewing machine. His eyes were slightly lopsided, and there was a large scar that ran around the top of his head. He had similar scars around his wrists and, all told, he looked a little bit like a human jigsaw puzzle.

To top it all off, he was only as tall as Trixie's waist. A stack of stools balanced unevenly on top of each other made it clear how he had managed to look out of the hatch in the door.

"My name is Grimsby." The tiny man lisped as he spoke. Trixie was quite taken aback by the sight but did her very best to hide her shock. She had no intention of appearing rude and making enemies so early on. He had clearly noticed them both staring as he continued: "I am the caretaker. I have a lot of accidents here. Sometimes the young ladies and gentlemen like to leave little traps for me. I patch myself up the best I can. It's all fun and games, I assure you."

Trixie went to say, "That's awful," but the mismatched gentleman coughed politely and stepped forwards to take the suitcase from her mum. The handle reached far above his head and he had to jump to grab hold of it. For a short while, he hung limply before finally the case tipped back and he was able to drag it away into the main building.

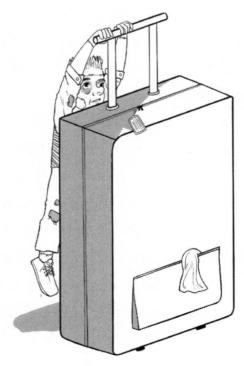

Unsure of what else to do, Trixie's mum gave her a hug and a pat on the back.

"Well, my dear," she said awkwardly, "I'm sure you will have a very nice time here. It looks… lovely." she finished uncertainly.

"Are you really very sure that I have to stay?" asked Trixie optimistically.

"Trixie, we have been through this far too many times. You really must do your very best to make the most of it. Besides, your bedroom is now a training room for the kittens. You know how much they need the space to unwind in after a hard day.

"Now, I must be going. I promised Mrs Burbage that I would pick up some of Mr Burbage's cream. His rash is back and he is starting to smell again."

Without another word, her mum turned and left Trixie all alone at the entrance to her new school. You can imagine just how scared she was as she stood there waiting to be told what to do.

Luckily for Trixie, she didn't have to wait for too long before a very tall, very fat woman emerged from the shadows. She was dressed head to toe in a flowing black dress that did nothing to hide just how large she really was and instead just made her look rather like a cannonball. Her long black hair was scraped back from her forehead and was pinned into a fierce bun. Her eyes were a brilliant shade of red that matched her lips and several of her teeth were rather longer and certainly sharper than Trixie felt comfortable with.

The woman was quite clearly a Vampire.

The whole scary effect was slightly ruined by the fact that she had a bright pink shawl decorated with yellow ducks wrapped around her shoulders and that her vivid red lips were parted in a warm and welcoming smile. There was a well-used tissue poking out of her sleeve and a whistle hung on a piece of string around her neck.

She was also sporting a pair of large glasses that magnified her eyes and made them look too big for her head. When she spoke, her voice had the soft, patient quality of those used to explaining things over and again to other people's children.

"Welcome!" the Vampire gushed as she grabbed

Trixie by the shoulders and knelt down so that she was face to face. Trixie heard the lady's knees creak under the strain. "Welcome to Monroe's Academy for the Different! Or Monstacademy as the children are calling it nowadays! We do try to move with the times, even if some of us are over three-hundred years old! I am Miss Flopsbottom, and I am the headmistress here! It really is a pleasure to have you join us Trixie. I just know that you will have the best time here. All of the other children are so eager to meet you. You are, after all, the very first *ordinary* person to attend Monstacademy!"

Trixie would soon learn just how *different* the other children were.

CHAPTER 3

Poodles and Parsnips

It turned out that not all of the children at Monstacademy were excited to have a normal child in their form. Trixie really did stick out like a sore thumb.

On her first day, she saw just how many different types of monster there were: Vampires and Werewolves of course, along with the less monstrous Witches and Wizards. But there were also a few Gargoyles, a scrawny boy who smelt of fish and lived under a tree who Trixie eventually found out was a Goblin, a girl who was half cat and a very hairy giant of a boy who claimed to be the great-great-great-great-grandson of Bigfoot.

Trixie spent the first few weeks of the term alone trying her best to stay out of trouble. It didn't matter how hard she tried, though. Trouble always seemed to find her.

Whilst Miss Flopsbottom was kind enough, most of the class teachers were less so. In fact, some of them were positively mean and nasty!

One of the worst teachers of all was Mr Snickletinkle the science teacher. He was a very old and very wiry Vampire. Everyone said that when it was a full moon, he would turn into a bat and drink the blood of the child that he disliked the most. Trixie hoped that this wasn't true. She suspected she'd be first course on his menu.

Trixie spent most of Mr Snickletinkle's lessons trying to mix exciting potions from a battered old textbook, often with disastrous results. Most of the other monsters had attended the Monster Elementary Starter School (M.E.S.S for short) and had lots of practise with this kind of thing. Trixie was very jealous of how easy the other children found it. Theirs were often perfect. Trixie's, on the other hand, nearly always ended up exploding or bubbling over in a frothy mess.

On one memorable occasion, Trixie had slipped

whilst chopping up a cup of snake's eyes and had cut the tip of her finger. Without thinking, she had approached Mr Snickletinkle for a sticking plaster. She'd completely forgotten the effect that blood has on Vampires of any age and the sight of hers leaking from the tip of her finger had been rather too much for him to handle and he'd had to go home for a lie up (you or I might go for a lie down, but then we don't sleep hanging from the ceiling like a bat). After that, he never really warmed to Trixie.

It wasn't just the teachers who disliked Trixie, either. Trixie was unpopular with most of the other children. They didn't like the fact that she was different to themselves and was rather boring, not having any special powers or the like, but she knew that they were also getting upset about the fact that lots of their lessons were disrupted by Trixie's clumsiness.

If we found ourselves in a school where nobody liked us and where we were so very different to all of the other children, you or I might ask our mum or dad to send us to another school.

Trixie didn't have that choice, of course, because she hadn't spoken to her mum since she had dropped her off. She knew that she would have to wait until Christmas and the end of term before she could even think about putting in a formal complaint.

Had Trixie continued to be friendless until

Christmas, she may well have had stern words with her mum, moved to a different school and the ending to this story may well have been very different.

Luckily for all of us, Trixie wasn't friendless for very much longer. Her situation changed one morning during poetry with Miss Tinkleton in the middle of a very cold and windy October. They were deep into a lesson about the work of William Wordsworth when Miss Brimstone, the deputy headmistress, had stuck her head through the door and requested Trixie's attention in the corridor.

Halloween was on the horizon, and the whole school was preparing for the biggest celebration of their school year. Each year Monstacademy held a Halloween Bash that included a festive parade through the town along with a formal dance for the children.

As organiser of the whole Bash, Miss Brimstone was responsible for making sure that everything went without a hitch. Right now, she dragged Trixie by her shoulder and swept her into the corridor.

"Trixie!" she wailed. Miss Brimstone was a Banshee, and so she wailed everything that she said. "I really don't like you." Trixie wasn't surprised but it still wasn't nice to hear. "You don't belong at Monroe's, and I intend to see to it that you don't stick around.

"However, right now I may as well make use of you. I see that you haven't been given a job for the Halloween Bash. How ever did that happen?" Trixie shrugged. She had no idea and wasn't particularly bothered.

"Well, as a first year you really shouldn't be given anything important. Heaven knows what kind of trouble you could cause. Unfortunately, all of the positions sweeping up spiders' webs or chasing the mice out of the kitchen have been taken."

Miss Brimstone curled her nose up, giving Trixie the impression that she could smell something rather foul in the air. "Luckily for you, I have one space left on the banner-making team. This really is a very, very important job, Trixie. The Great

Unfurling of the banner is the key moment in the whole Parade.

"The Parade itself is the talk of the town. People come from miles around. It's a way for us to show the rest of the town that we really *aren't* that scary. Surely when you were…before you came *here*, you saw the Parade?"

Trixie hadn't. She and her friends had been dead set against it. They'd wanted nothing to do with the *freaks* up at the castle on the hill. They'd made jokes and laughed about how scary they must be. They didn't seem so funny now. She shook her head.

"Are you sure that you can cope with this responsibility?" Miss Brimstone didn't wait for Trixie to reply before continuing. "There are only two other people doing it, and frankly they need the help. They are snivelling first-years as well, but we just can't take any of the others away from their jobs. The older children all have coursework to do amongst other things. Goodness knows how we'll ever be finished on time!"

Trixie stood and listened as Miss Brimstone rattled off a seemingly endless list of reasons about why first years were being given such an important task. Eventually, the teacher seemed to remember that Trixie was there and pulled herself up to her full, haughty height.

"Make your way to the cellar beneath the great hall at lunchtime and get to work!" With that, the Banshee had flown away down the corridor, and Trixie had made her way back into her classroom slightly more confused than when she'd left.

That lunchtime, Trixie made her way down beneath the school and into the depths of the hall beneath. To get to the cellar, she had to leave the main dormitory building and head across the courtyard and through the hall. She couldn't shake the feeling that she was being followed all of the way, but each time she turned around, there was nothing there.

"Stop being so silly!" she muttered to herself over and over again. "All the talk of monsters has gone to your head!"

Soon, Trixie had made her way across the main hall and carefully descended the small flight of steps to the cellar. As she stepped into the room, she was surprised to see a young girl already working away in the clean and surprisingly well-lit cellar. The girl had long, dark hair and was wearing a black cape over the customary grey school uniform. Trixie recognised her as one of the Vampires from her science class.

"Monroe's Academy. That's what it needs to say. Make sure we spell it correctly. I'd hate to miss a letter out," said the Vampire over her shoulder as soon as Trixie entered. Her voice was clipped but friendly enough and had the posh, rolled sounds of the very wealthiest of families.

"Oh, hello," she said a little deflated as she turned around and saw that it was Trixie. "I thought you were Colin. He's been helping me, but he's jolly late today."

"Sorry." said Trixie. She didn't know what else to say. "Miss Brimstone sent me. She said you needed help," Trixie offered, suddenly remembering why she was there.

"Well, we don't need any help thank you," the Vampire replied haughtily. "And certainly not from you." Trixie looked shocked before she realised that the girl was pointing past her and back towards the doorway. As she turned a scruffy-looking boy draped in a far-too-big wizard's robe sniggered and bolted back up the stairs.

"Sorry about that. That was Heston Gobswaddle. He's supposed to be a Wizard, but he's terrible at everything except for turning people into squirrels. He's always up to no good as well. I bet he was down here trying to figure out how we are getting on. You know, really he should be a fourth-year, but he's so dim-witted he keeps having to repeat the second year!

"Anyway, we don't need help. But, if Miss Brimstone sent you then I suppose you had better make yourself useful. Gloria." The Vampire extended her hand awkwardly.

"Pardon?" asked Trixie, holding it limply and confused by the sudden change of direction.

"I'm Gloria. Gloria Toothsome. I'm a Vampire. I know who you are, of course. Everybody knows Trixie the Ordinary." Trixie felt herself blushing from her toes to her cheeks. She'd heard some of the other children call her that behind her back but had tried to ignore it.

"Don't worry," Gloria continued in a more reassuring voice. "Nobody likes me, either. I'm not like the others. Neither is Colin. That's why getting this right is so important. If we make this the biggest, most amazing banner Monroe's has ever seen then the others will just have to like us."

"Why don't they like you or Colin?" asked Trixie, eager to take the conversation away from her.

"Well, I'm not like the other Vampires. I'm a vegetarian, you see. I don't like blood. It's too icky. Even the black pudding that they serve us in the canteen. I much prefer to bite into a good parsnip!" The young Vampire pulled a well-chewed vegetable from her pocket to illustrate her point. "I always carry one around with me in case I need a light bite!" Gloria smiled toothfully. "The other Vampires don't like that. They say it makes me weak. I say, if they want to drink icky, sticky blood and have horrible red-stained teeth, then that's up to them, but I'm not."

"So, you're a vege*scarian*?" Trixie couldn't help herself and started to giggle. Luckily, Gloria found it equally as funny, and they were soon patting each other on the back trying to calm down.

Eventually, Trixie wiped the tears from her eyes and asked "And what about Colin?"

"What about Colin?" Trixie turned towards the door at the sound of the cheerful voice and watched as a young boy bounded in. At least, he looked like a young boy, but it is normally quite impossible for a boy of any age to grow the amount of hair that covered Colin from head to toe. Even his fingers were hairy. The hair was short and hugged his body closely, but there was no getting away from the fact that he was a very hairy young thing. He really did bound as well. There was something about the way he moved that made Trixie want to shout out "Fetch!".

"Sorry about the hair." He laughed as he noticed Trixie staring at him. "It's part of my curse. I'm Colin. Colin Curlyton."

"Your curse?" Trixie asked curiously as she shook his hand gently.

"Well, I'm a Werewolf. Sort of. Most Werewolves only get really hairy when they turn into a wolf at the full moon. Something went wrong when I was born though, I'm hairier than normal all of the time."

"Oh, that must be dreadfully uncomfortable!" said Trixie. She meant it, too. She knew just how uncomfortable it was when the hair on her head grew too long and kept flicking in front of her eyes.

"That's not the worst part," Colin said. "You know how I said most Werewolves turn into a wolf at the full moon?" Trixie nodded. Gloria giggled to herself in the background and had to cover her mouth with her hand. "Most Werewolves have nice long, shiny hair and turn into a glorious, strong wolf. Not me. Whenever it's a full moon near me, I turn into…a poodle!" Gloria couldn't contain herself anymore and once again burst into fits of giggles. Eventually Trixie saw Colin break into a smile and joined in with the laughter.

From that point on, the three of them were best friends.

CHAPTER 4

Food for Thought

I bet that everybody who goes to your school is more or less perfectly ordinary. There is probably one boy who picks his nose too often or who trumps rather too loudly when your teacher is talking. Or there might be a girl who is much too chatty or giggles at even the most unfunny of things. Compared to the pupils who attended Monstacademy, the children in your class are positively dull.

Take, for instance, the school toilets. How do you go to the toilet? Don't worry. You don't need to answer. We know just how you go to the toilet. However, how do you think that a Werewolf goes to the toilet when they've turned into a wolf (or a poodle if they are Colin)? What about poor Gladys, the girl who turned into a cat every third Thursday and liked to chase mice and lick her paws? She needed a giant litter box in the corner of the room. How embarrassing!

It doesn't even bear thinking about when it came to sleeping arrangements. Trixie was perfectly happy with her lumpy bed that smelt slightly of feet, but Gloria left her bed alone and had a special rail installed in the ceiling so that she could hang upside down like her Vampire family back home.

Colin had a bed but used his small wicker basket once a month. There was a pink bone in the corner that squeaked when he chewed it. The Banshees slept on the rooftops, the Ghosts didn't bother to sleep and the Bogie-monsters slept underneath each other's beds.

All of these differences made it extra difficult for Trixie in the first few weeks. Trixie tried her best to fit in. It helped now that she had friends and that she felt like she was doing something useful with the Halloween banner, but the toilets and beds weren't the worst part of attending Monstacademy. Mealtimes were much worse.

Trixie was the first ordinary person that had ever attended Monstacademy. When she had first started, the cook had hidden away in the cupboard for a day and had what Miss Flopsbottom referred to as Hysterics. He had refused to come out until Trixie promised to try at least some of the food that he cooked. In fact, most of the food was acceptable if not delicious and Trixie was happy to eat it. It was the food specifically cooked for some of the other children that was so hard to stomach.

The other children ate such things as:

Lumps of raw steak for the Werewolves

Live sheep for the Vampires to snack on (or black pudding for the ones who preferred to chew their meals)

Raw fish for Gladys

Eyeball soup for the Banshees

The ghosts of various animals for the Ghosts and Ghouls (Trixie never did get used to the sight of a ghostly pig lying on a silver platter.)

In the end, Trixie found that the best way to get through mealtimes was to take her own plate of food and sit in a corner with Gloria and Colin. Gloria was a vegetarian and refused to sit near raw meat anyway, and Colin had to eat dry dog biscuits once a month, and the other children laughed at him until he'd moved away.

"Look at them all, chewing on their horrible meat and drinking the blood of those poor sheep. Sometimes, I really hate being a Vampire," Gloria had said one day whilst she sat and chewed sadly on yet another parsnip. Trixie was beginning to realise that Gloria always chewed on a parsnip whenever she was worried or angry.

The three of them had found that as winter

approached the basement was getting very cold indeed and they were spending more and more time in the dinner hall. Trixie didn't dare to think just how far behind they were on the banner.

Elsewhere in the hall, the sound of the other Vampires drinking their dinner sounded a lot like somebody trying to get the last bit of milkshake from the bottom of a cup. It made Trixie feel sick and quite put her off her potatoes. It was nearly always potatoes. They were cheap and easy to cook and, Trixie suspected, were one of the few ordinary foods that the chef was happy cooking.

"Come on, we really should get back to the banner. I've got loads of my letters to finish." Trixie tried to hurry the others along but she shared their reluctance to move. It really was nice and warm.

"It's fine." Colin sounded muffled with a mouthful of trifle. "We'll just take them up to our rooms and finish them the night before if we need to. Besides, there's loads of time before the Parade. Here, have some trifle."

Trixie pushed his hand away and turned instead

to the more reliable Gloria. Even she wasn't keen on leaving the hall just yet.

"Maybe in a minute. Colin's right. There is quite a lot of time left."

Despite the horrible food, disgusting sounds and revolting smells, they often found themselves sat in the hall for the whole of lunchtime, the incredibly important banner all but forgotten down in the cold basement.

Getting used to the dinner hall was very nearly the hardest thing that Trixie had to get used to during her time at Monstacademy. She would soon find out that there were worse things in life than hungry Vampires.

CHAPTER 5

The Worst Monster in School

It wasn't long after yet another lunchtime had passed without any more work being done on the banner, and Trixie was cowering in the middle of a playing field at the bottom of the grassy hill that led away to the back of Monstacademy. She was being given a lesson in just how difficult it was to attend a school for the different.

"You are *easily* the worst monster in school, Trixie Grimble!"

Trixie shuddered and tried to hide herself away from the rest of the class. The shrieking voice that seemed to fill the entire hillside belonged to a young Werewolf named Esme Furfang. On a normal day, Esme was a pretty, popular girl who, other than her pointed ears and slightly hairy arms, looked like any other girl Trixie had ever met. Right now though, you could be forgiven for thinking that she was in fact a hideous river monster. She was soaking wet and covered head to toe in slimy, smelly pond weed. This was because she had just stepped out of the middle of a large pond.

The pond and the surrounding fields were normally out of bounds for the pupils, but they had been allowed to play there today as part of their games lesson with Mr Fetch. Mr Fetch was a Werewolf and lots of his lessons involved balls in some shape or other, and he often loved to join in.

Today was no exception. Trixie and her class had all made their way down to the large grass field to play a game of Snaffleball. You may never have played Snaffleball before. Trixie Grimble certainly hadn't.

A Snaffleball court is very similar to a tennis court but is roughly twice as large. The net across the middle is taller than a grown-up, and the ball is about the same size as a small football. It is also very soft and made of sponge. They are normally orange.

There is a bucket that sits on the back line on each side of the court. To score a point each team much try to get the ball into the bucket on the opposite side of the court. To help them with this they have one player, a Snaffler, who is allowed onto the other side of the court. He or she is the only player that is allowed to catch the ball.

All of the other players (six on each side of the court) must try to keep the ball moving backwards and forwards over the net using any part of their body, a bit like volleyball. If you are anything like me, then your brain is probably hurting trying to understand all of those rules.

If you really want to understand it properly then I suggest you ask your teacher if you can play a game of Snaffleball in your next gym lesson.

If it makes you feel any better, Trixie found it rather confusing as well. That really was only the start of her problems, though. Trixie wasn't very good at sports and really struggled to throw and catch. Maybe you are the same. It's not a nice feeling when your teacher is barking at you to throw the ball harder, faster or straighter when you are already trying your hardest.

Over the course of the game the rules had become slightly clearer. You were allowed to pick the ball up if it bounced once, but if it bounced twice you had to start the round again, kicking the ball was allowed, but if it landed in the basket it didn't count. And running into your own teammate was likely to make the rest of your team very angry. Trixie found this out the hard way very early on.

To avoid any more of this embarrassment, Trixie had spent the rest of the game trying to stay out of trouble at the back of the court whilst her teammates huffed and puffed and kicked and volleyed and whacked and thwacked the ball to and fro.

Then it happened. Henrietta Roche, a Gargoyle on an exchange trip from Honolulu, smacked the ball with all her might high over the net. Trixie watched as it flew in slow motion towards her. For a long time, it seemed to hang in the air and she wondered if it might have forgotten to fall back down but, soon enough, gravity took hold and it fell back down to earth right in front of her.

Without thinking, Trixie swung an arm and hit the soft ball as hard as she could. If she had hit the ball over the net, the moment would have passed with nothing more than a slight bead of sweat appearing on Trixie's forehead.

The ball didn't go over the net, though. The ball ricocheted off her hand and flew straight out of the court and bounced away towards the large, still pond. A family of ducks quacked in anger as it rolled down the bank, picking up speed as it went, and bounced straight through their nest.

"So the ball will get a little wet!" I hear you crying. "There are far worse things that could happen!" And under normal circumstances, you would be correct. Unfortunately, Esme Furfang was feeling particularly wolf-like on this day. If you are lucky enough to own a dog, you will know just how excited they get when they see a ball being thrown.

It is all they can do not to explode with excitement as they chase it down. A young girl who is feeling particularly wolf-like has much the same reaction. So as soon as poor Trixie had thwacked the ball out of the court, Esme had yelped out loud and given chase. Her tongue flapped from the corner of her mouth like a Labrador as she panted and puffed towards her prize.

Unluckily for Esme, the ball landed in the pond with a soft squelch at much the same time as she

caught up with it. You know yourself that when you are running your very fastest, especially if you are chasing something, it is very difficult to stop suddenly, and so Esme found herself falling headfirst into the pond with an enormous splash.

The family of ducks were definitely angry and decided to take their anger out on the poor girl by flapping and pecking at her bottom every time that it bobbed above the surface. You can imagine how angry this made her!

And so it was that when Esme finally emerged

from the pond she was soaking wet and covered in stinking, straggly pond weed. Trixie felt awful and tried her best to apologise to the Werewolf as she trudged back towards the court with the soft ball held between her teeth.

"Ooh are *eefily* ve wrft monfter in ftool!" Esme mumbled.

"Pardon?" asked Trixie apologetically.

Esme spat the ball out of her mouth and turned to look at Trixie angrily.

"You are *easily* the worst monster in school, Trixie Grimble!"

And that was the end of the matter. Esme never liked Trixie after that, particularly after the other children started calling her Pond Girl. After a week, Trixie stopped trying to say sorry and just made sure that she avoided Esme whenever she could.

CHAPTER 6

A Lesson in Disaster

With only two weeks to go until the Halloween Bash, the preparations were going into overdrive. The whole school was getting into the Halloween spirit, and everybody was talking about all of the fun things that would be happening in the coming weeks.

Practice pumpkins were quickly piling up outside each of the dormitories as children worked their way towards a winning design for the pumpkin showcase.

Normally, Trixie would have been deciding on a fancy dress costume about now. There were dress-up days at school to think about and, of course, trick-or-treating to be done. She was sad that she wouldn't get chance to do that this year, but it wasn't long before she found herself distracted by the enormous amount of work that still needed to be done for the parade.

Trixie, Gloria and Colin were spending all of their free time making sure that their banner was in tip-top condition. They'd painted each letter onto a giant wooden triangle that would be threaded onto a thick rope on the day of the Parade. As well as the letters, each section was being decorated with something suitably spooky.

Trixie was particularly proud of a detailed spider's web that she had painted using silver paint and a very fine brush. She'd added a scary spider made from a ball of wool that would hang down below the banner and scare everyone who walked past.

Gloria had decorated one of the letters with a Wicked Witch complete with green skin and a giant boil on the end of her nose. She secretly hoped that Agnes Dimpiddle, a mean Witch in their form who had often picked on Gloria, would see it and be rather upset at the likeness.

Colin had painted a poodle having a wee against the letter C. He'd found it absolutely hilarious and had refused every attempt by Gloria to get him to paint over it. In the end, Gloria had just tutted and said something about boys being so very silly. Trixie had kept quiet. She'd found it almost as funny as Colin had.

Every now and again they would come back to the cellar to find things in slightly different positions, and more than once they'd even caught Heston Gobswaddle running away from the cellar door.

"I'm telling you, he's up to no good!" Colin had

growled after he'd chased Heston away.

"We'll need to keep a closer eye on him and try to get a key for the cellar door. The last thing we need is him ruining our beautiful work," agreed Gloria.

There were still a lot of letters left to paint, and so Trixie often found her mind wandering during lessons. She liked to think about what scary pictures she was going to paint that lunchtime and sometimes lost track entirely of what was being said.

I imagine that sometimes you don't pay attention in class, either. Maybe your teacher is droning on about something unimportant again or your head-teacher is giving you yet another boring assembly on how to tie your shoelaces.

Whatever it might be, there has probably been a time when your mind has wandered away to do something more interesting. Should this ever happen to you, you will know that the worst that might ever happen is that you start to snore loudly and your teacher or head-teacher gives you a jolly good telling off.

At Monstacademy, however, the lessons are a little bit different. As we already know, the science lessons were often spent making potions, but the other lessons were rather more interesting as well.

Poetry was taught by the Zombies of the people who first wrote them, maths was taught by an old Wizard who couldn't remember where he left his wooden staff and whose moustache crackled with dangerous raw magic and the history lessons were taught by Mr Spike, a Mummy from Ancient Egypt who loved nothing more than to terrify the children with stories from beyond the grave.

This lesson though, the one in which Trixie had so haphazardly let her mind wander, was Hide and Seek. Their weekly lessons in Hide and Seek were designed to encourage the children to get out into the fresh air and to think about good places to hide and how to run away, something that Monstacademy knew the children might unfortunately need to do when out in the real world where ordinary members of the public couldn't be trusted not to turn up at your door with a polite knock and a pitchfork.

Trixie's teacher for Hide and Seek was Mr Tiddlesnot and he was a Gnome. This meant that he was very small and very good at hiding in very small spaces. He normally won. Trixie didn't see the point in Hide and Seek as she would never have to hide when she was older, and so she allowed herself to wander around the school playing fields not really looking where she was going.

It was for exactly that reason that Trixie didn't realise that she had wandered into the corner of the field where children were not supposed to play. The corner of the field that contained the unmarked old well dug deep into the soft ground. I expect you can imagine what happened next. Quite clumsily indeed, Trixie tripped over the edge of the well and her feet flew into the air. She fell bottom-first down into the hole and is only still alive today because the bottom of the well was filled with very soft mud.

Had it been filled with rocks or water, as many

old wells are, then quite frankly I wouldn't have given her much chance of making it out alive.

Luckily for Trixie, and indeed this story, she did survive the fall and merely landed with a wet squelch. Her first thought was to shout out to attract attention to herself, but she could already hear a group of voices wandering over to the top of the well and so she decided to wait until they were closer before asking them for a little help.

When the voices reached the top of the well she was concerned when she recognised them as Heston Gobswaddle and his miserable friends. Gloria and Colin had been right when they said Heston was a bad egg. He was often up to mischief, but they knew that there was nothing that they could do.

For some reason, Miss Brimstone had taken quite a shine to Heston, and he had become a bit of a teacher's pet as well as a giant twit. Trixie would have suspected that he'd placed her under some sort of spell if she hadn't known just how dim he was.

Everybody knew that he wasn't very clever and didn't know many spells, but that didn't matter because nobody wanted to spend their life as a squirrel and so everybody was especially nice to Heston and his friends, Kevin Thimblenose, a boy who had a pumpkin for head after an unfortunate magical accident when he was a child, and Dilbert Trompton, a Ghost.

Dilbert had been killed by an angry gorilla at the local zoo many years before and now spent his days acting like one. Trixie could not have asked for worse saviours. Luckily, they didn't seem to have noticed her. Overhead, they were conducting their own private conversation.

"It'll definitely work guys. That stupid parade is the best time to get revenge on all of the *freaks* down in the town. They won't know what hit them! All their years trick-or-treating and making fun of us will finally come back to bite them in the bottom. Even the school motto agrees with me."

Trixie started to panic.

So that was why he was spying on us, she thought. *He wants to do something at the Parade, and messing up our banner would be the perfect way!*

"But, Heston." That was definitely the ape-like voice of Dilbert. "They won't let us anywhere near them to do it. They hate people like us."

"Don't worry, my monkey-loving friend. Leave that to me!"

Trixie heard them walking away but left it a good while before shouting for help. Eventually, Gloria and Colin stopped playing Hide and Seek for long enough to stroll over and pull her out on the end of a long piece of rope. On the way back to the classroom, Trixie told them all about what she had heard.

CHAPTER 7

The Wooden Chest

Now I don't know about you, but if I'd spent nearly an hour stuck down a well, I would want to take a nice hot bath and maybe have a lovely bowl of soup to steady my nerves. It says something about Trixie's character that all she wanted to do was to work out what Heston, Kevin and Dilbert were up to.

By the time that Trixie, Gloria and Colin had arrived back at the main school building they had made up their minds to investigate just what the terrible threesome were up to.

Their plan was to make their way to the boys' bedrooms to see if they could find any evidence to suggest what devious devilment they were plotting.

The second-year dormitories were on the other side of the school to Trixie's, so it took them quite a while to find their way through the meandering corridors and across the main courtyard. They were slowed down even more by their desire to arrive undetected, and so they spent as much time as they could skulking along the walls in the shadows. At one point, Trixie was convinced that she saw Miss Brimstone watching them from one of the windows high up in one of the stone towers, but as soon as she looked harder the shadow disappeared.

Eventually they stood outside the dark wooden door that they knew led to the bedroom of the second-year boys. Taking a deep breath, Gloria turned the handle and they stepped inside. It was the middle of the day, and so all of the children were down in the main building making their way to their next lesson, but Trixie, Gloria and Colin still felt goosebumps rise up on the back of their necks.

Like all of the bedrooms at Monstacademy, this one was a long, thin dormitory that had four beds lined up along each long wall. Like all of the bedrooms occupied by boys of any age, it also smelt of old socks and too many beans. At the foot of each bed was a heavy wooden chest for personal belongings, and there was just enough room to walk between them.

Each bed was dressed with the same dark red bedspread and pillowcases and the school crest was hung above the head of each. At the end of the long room, a tall window looked out over the school grounds and was deep enough for someone to sit on the windowsill and read a book in comfort, should a child choose to do so.

"Colin, you keep an eye on the door and me and Trixie will split up and look under each of the beds. As soon as we find Heston's, we'll have a look inside his chest and see what he's got planned."

Colin moaned about being disappointed about not to be able to dig around himself but nevertheless took himself to the door and opened it a crack to look out onto the corridor beyond. He started to pick his nose for something to do.

School rules said that every child must keep the area underneath their bed clean and tidy. As with all school rules, it had been disobeyed almost immediately. The underside of each of the second year's beds was a nest of old underpants and vests, mouldy socks and half-eaten bars of chocolate smuggled into the school from the village below. It was through this stench-filled swamp that Trixie and Gloria found themselves swimming. Despite their best efforts, they struggled to find anything of interest. It wasn't until they reached the other end of the room that they finally stumbled upon Heston's bed. His name was carved into his trunk along with about a dozen threats to anyone foolish enough to look inside.

Gloria and Trixie looked inside.

They saw what was inside the trunk at the same time as they heard a muffled grunt from behind them. Dragging their eyes away from their shocking discovery, they were dismayed to see Colin struggling to break free from Kevin Thimblenose's grip. It didn't matter how often Trixie saw Kevin, she still couldn't stop gawping at his round, orange pumpkin head.

"What happened?" scalded Gloria. "You were supposed to be keeping a lookout!"

Colin had the decency to look bashful. "I just took my eyes off the door for a second. There was something under the bed that looked interesting."

"Trust me," Trixie grumbled. "I've been under there and there is nothing interesting at all unless you consider Heath Humperdink's dirty pants interesting."

"Stop it! All of you!" Kevin interrupted. "What are you doing in Heston's chest? I'm going to fetch him. He'll deal with you" His crooked pumpkin smile grew wider. He clearly felt like he'd won the battle. "Yeah, that's right. You lot stay here, and I'll go and get Heston."

"What if we leave?" asked Colin, unable to help himself. This seemed to confuse Kevin who didn't seem like the quickest thinker in the world.

"Listen, Kevin," Gloria butted in before their captor had time to work out what to do. "If you tell Heston, we'll just have to tell everyone what we've seen in that box, won't we? Why don't you just let us go peacefully and we can forget all about this?" Kevin seemed unsure. "Just think, Kevin. How annoyed will Heston be if his big secret gets out because of you?" That seemed to swing it for him. He relaxed his grip on Colin who immediately turned around and kicked him hard between the legs. Before he could get back up, the three of them raced through the door and back out into the school courtyard.

"What was in the box?" gasped Colin when they finally stopped under the shadow of a tall oak tree. "It must have been serious?"

"There were loads of animals in there," wheezed Trixie, who was regretting not spending more time keeping fit.

"What, bugs and things?"

"No, bigger animals." Gloria had obviously spent more time staying in shape and was staring at the other two with a mixture of embarrassment and pity. "Foxes, badgers, squirrels and things like that. I'm sure I even saw an elephant and a giraffe in there."

"Don't be ridiculous!" Colin laughed. "There's no way that even one of those animals could fit into that chest, let alone all of those."

"That's the thing, though," whispered Trixie in case anyone was listening in. "All of them had been shrunk down to the size of toys. They were still moving around and alive and everything, just really, really small."

"Why would he have a load of small animals in a chest?" asked Colin.

"Who knows," sighed Gloria, "but we better get to the bottom of it and quickly."

CHAPTER 8

The Parade

As it happened, it was a while before they managed to get any closer to working out why Heston had a trunk full of tiny animals. Halloween soon rolled around. Before they knew it, it was time for the annual Halloween Parade.

Each year the Parade wound its way down from Monstacademy and into and through the town of Wexbridge below. It was a way for the Vampires to step out of their coffins, the Bogie-boys and -girls to come out from under the beds and the Werewolves to let their hair down.

For Trixie, it was a reminder of her old life. She found that she'd stopped missing it quite a while ago, particularly now that she had a couple of firm friends.

If you've ever been to a parade, and I've been to quite a few in my time, you will know that they are noisy, colourful and fun places to be, especially during the warm summer months. As this particular parade was taking place on Halloween, the weather did very well to stay dry and all of the children were thoroughly enjoying their slow ride through the closed-off roads on their floats.

Trixie, Gloria and Colin were on the third float from the front, behind the final year students who looked very serious in their long, dark robes and behind the teacher's float where Miss Flopsbottom and the rest of the faculty were keeping a very close eye on the rolled-up banner that hung above Trixie's head.

Miss Brimstone wore a particularly sour frown and kept her eyes fixed firmly on Trixie. The Parade was to be the first great-unfurling of the new banner, and Miss Flopsbottom had stressed the importance of such an occasion that very morning.

Even having a banner to unfurl in the first place had been an achievement. What with one thing and another and the mystery surrounding Heston's plan, Trixie, Gloria and Colin had quite neglected their duties and had ended up having to throw the banner together at the last minute in the dark the night before the Parade.

It'll be fine, Trixie reassured herself. *It has to be fine.*

Trixie soon forgot the hastily prepared banner as she spotted an enormous, flamboyant float approaching from the other end of the high street.

It was customary for the floats of Monstacademy to meet the floats of Cromley's Royal Academy for the Zany Youth (or C.R.A.Z.Y as their school crest read) along the route. Cromley's was another school for those different to the rest of the society and was situated far away on the other side of a neighbouring county. Their nickname was The Ghoul School.

Normally, if the parade had been timed correctly, the floats would meet in the middle of the high street and there they would both unfurl their school banners and cheer for each other before continuing on their journey.

Even from this distance, Trixie could make out the bright purple and silver uniforms of the Ghoul School students and their teachers. They looked sharp in the autumn sunlight and their floats were all so much better than Monstacademy's. Trixie was sure that the other Monstacademy students had tried their best, but their floats were all a little drab and unimpressive compared to the splendour of their counterparts.

Before long, the float bearing Cromley's banner had pulled up alongside Trixie's. This was the moment they had all been waiting for. The crowd fell silent as I'm quite sure you would have had you been there. Certain situations like this just demand silence. Even the babies stopped crying and the dogs stopped barking.

Trixie jumped as the silence was momentarily broken by a trumpet player sounding a few notes to signal the beginning of the Great Unfurling.

As the visitors, Cromley's went first. There was a snap like a whip as the long rope that held their banner was pulled free. The beautifully gilded letters fluttered gently in the calm breeze before being pulled tight between two poles that pointed skywards. Each letter was surrounded with gold filigree. The whole thing had been sprinkled with just the right amount of gold glitter, and it took Trixie's breath away. The audience seemed to agree, and there was a loud cheer and round of applause before silence fell again. Trixie felt suddenly guilty for their crude drawings.

Trixie took a deep breath and pulled on her own rope and watched with a smile as Monroe's banner slowly unfurled. She pulled the rope tight to string the banner between the two tall poles attached to their own float and allowed herself a sigh of relief.

From where she was stood, Trixie could only make out the back of the banner, but she was happy that they had taken the time to decorate the reverse of each of the letters as well, even the audience behind their banner would have something to look at.

Something wasn't right though. The audience weren't cheering and they weren't clapping. Gloria and Colin, who had a better view of the front of the banner had turned their backs on Trixie and were trying their hardest to stifle a laugh.

Trixie looked over to the teachers' float for support, but the look on Miss Flopsbottom's face was one of despair and disappointment. Miss Brimstone was smiling a tight, hard smile that curved slightly at the corners of her mouth. Fearing the worst, Trixie stepped forward and looked up at the front of the banner. The banner that was supposed to display the venerable name of the school, Monroe's Academy.

She read it. She read it again.

Dreamy Mooncase!

Trixie screamed. She shouted. She sobbed. And then she fell silent.

Miss Flopsbottom's voice seemed to come from another planet, but when it arrived it did so with a gentle force that snapped Trixie and her friends out of their horrific nightmare. She ordered them from their float and sent them to wait in the audience with strict instructions to meet the rest of the students back at school once the parade was over. They made their way silently through the crowd who parted awkwardly to let them through.

There were a few polite coughs from amongst the crowd as the Parade slowly continued its journey.

Trixie, Gloria and Colin eventually pushed their way clear of the last few people and took a deep breath.

"So that's what Heston has been doing!" moaned Gloria. "I knew he was up to something. I'll give him such a hiding the next time I see him!"

"Maybe," muttered Colin, distracted by something.

"Maybe?" cursed Gloria. "Of course, it was him!"

"Well, obviously it was him." Colin dismissed his friend's anger with a wave of his hands. "But it doesn't make sense. Why go to all that trouble just to embarrass us? I don't think that messing with our banner was his main plan. That was probably just a bit of fun for him."

"Maybe he was worried about what we saw in his bedroom and wanted to get us expelled? Kevin would definitely have told him that he caught us snooping around and maybe he got scared that we'd find out what he was really up to? Maybe he panicked and wanted us out of the way?" Trixie wondered out loud.

"Shhh!" shushed Gloria. "What's that?"

They turned around slowly and found themselves at the entrance to a dark alleyway that ran between two tall buildings. The noise appeared to be coming from the other end of the passage. It sounded like people arguing whilst trying to keep their voices very quiet.

Slowly, they made their way into the alleyway. About halfway along, they were brought up suddenly by a louder argument. They ducked behind a couple of those horrible flip-top bins that you often find behind restaurants. Whoever was talking was on the other side. Trixie felt her heart pounding in her chest. She was sure that it was loud enough for everyone to hear.

Holding their breath, the trio edged their way to the front of the bin and peeked around. As soon as they heard the voices clearly, they ducked back behind the bin and cursed their bad luck. Trixie's hair stood up on the back of her neck. It was Heston and his two cronies. They didn't seem to be whispering now, and Trixie could hear everything that they were saying.

"And the potion will definitely work, will it?" grunted Dilbert.

"Yeah, 'cos, like, we don't want to kill them or anything." That was the nervous voice of Kevin.

"Listen, guys, you've seen the animals. The zookeepers didn't even see me sneaking them out of their cages. They were that small. I had them all in my bag! Just a few drops of this potion into the water jugs and all of those thirsty, *freaky*, *ordinary* people out there will be small enough to tread on. It'll be awesome!" Heston looked at the horrified faces of his friends. "Honestly, you two! I *won't* tread on them, of course. I'm not a monster. Well, obviously I *am*, but you get the point. Look, just so we know that it works, I've brought along an experiment."

Trixie stood on her tiptoes and glanced carefully over the top of the stinking bin. Heston had disappeared behind a large wooden crate but soon returned with a struggling bundle of fury. Trixie recognised it as Timothy Whipsnittle, a small boy who had been born half-werewolf (he still grew hairier at a full moon, but he just needed to have a shave rather than the whole, running around eating people thing that normal werewolves had to put up with). His hands were tied behind his back and he had a sock stuffed into his mouth, but his screams were still loud enough to make Trixie feel sick.

Gloria and Colin stood up to see what all the fuss was about and Trixie had to grab hold of Colin to hold him back.

"I'll teach him to pick on somebody smaller than him!" whispered Colin angrily as Gloria joined Trixie in holding him still behind the bin.

As they watched helplessly, Heston removed the sock from Timothy's mouth. Before he could scream, Heston poured a small amount of the clear potion down his throat. Timothy hiccupped, burped and then shrank. Trixie was surprised at how quickly it all happened. It wasn't like in a film where the person shrinks slowly. One minute he was normal size and then the next he was no bigger than a thimble.

Laughing to themselves, Heston and his henchmen scooped Timothy up and shoved him into Heston's bag along with the potion. Without looking back, they raced out of the alleyway and back towards the Parade.

Trixie, Gloria and Colin all shivered at the same time and looked at each other with horrified expressions. They knew what they had to do. Trouble or not, they needed to find Miss Flopsbottom and fast.

CHAPTER 9

The Plan

Suddenly it seemed as though there were thousands of people all fighting to keep Trixie away from the road and away from Miss Flopsbottom and the rest of the Parade.

Everywhere that Trixie looked she could see adults and children happily swigging back the free water that had been thoughtfully provided by Monstacademy.

She couldn't begin to imagine what people would think if they found out that somebody from the school had poisoned the water and given it to innocent people. There would be uproar! There would be pandemonium! Monstacademy would be shut down and they'd throw away the key to the bottom of the deepest ocean! Trixie couldn't allow that to happen.

They had to stop Heston and fast.

After what felt like hours, they finally managed to push their way to the front of the crowd and saw that they weren't too far behind the front of the Parade. With a lot of pushing and stepping on toes, they made their way to the very float from which they had so recently been expelled.

The unhelpful banner still hung from the poles and fluttered forlornly in the wind. Trixie tried not to look at it. Instead, she urged her friends to push even harder forwards, and they made their way to the teachers' float where they were met with disdainful scowls by all of the faculty.

Miss Brimstone looked as though Trixie's arrival had given her a foul taste in her mouth. Even Miss Flopsbottom, who was normally so nice to them all, looked utterly displeased to see them return. Their antics today had clearly pushed her too far. They felt bad that they'd managed to upset one of the nicest teachers at the school, but they didn't have time to dwell on that now.

"Miss Flopsbottom, you must stop the parade

and you must do it now!" Trixie shouted so loudly
that several adults in the crowd turned to see what
the commotion was about. Miss Flopsbottom
shushed her quickly.

"Trixie Grimble, do be careful what you say.
You have caused quite enough embarrassment for
Monroe's Academy for the Different for one day.
Please, do as you are told and go wait with the
crowd." The head teacher turned away and tried to
ignore the trio as they shouted for her attention.

"My dear Trixie," wailed Miss Brimstone with unabashed glee in her eyes, "you really are determined to leave our fine school in bad grace, it would appear. Is it not enough that you have deeply embarrassed poor Miss Flopsbottom? I mean, honestly, she will clearly be expelling you after this nonsense, but if you continue to harass her I really don't see why she wouldn't have you sent away to one of the dungeons underneath the school for endangering the safety of monsters everywhere. After all, this kind of thing often leads to riots!"

"Oh, I say!" exclaimed Miss Flopsbottom, jumping to Trixie's defence. "Let's not get ahead of ourselves talking about expelling children and dungeons and all that." Miss Brimstone sat back down with a scornful growl, defeated by the large headmistress who now turned back to Trixie. "What is it that is so important that you had to disobey a direct instruction to stay away from the crowd?"

"Heston Gobswaddle is planning on using a

potion to shrink all of the people in the crowd, Miss!" Colin shouted as loudly as he could over the noise of the crowd. He was loud enough for Miss Flopsbottom to hear, and Trixie was happy to see a look of doubt pass across her face. Heston's mischief was well known across the Academy and what Colin was saying was definitely believable. Miss Brimstone leant forward and whispered something into the headmistress's ear. Her look of doubt passed and her face changed to one of disbelief and anger.

What has that old hag said to her now? wondered Trixie as Miss Flopsbottom once again sent them to wait in the crowd.

Knowing that they were defeated, Trixie, Gloria and Colin made their way to the back and sat down with their backs against a wall. Trixie was shocked to hear Gloria sobbing quietly as she sat next to her.

"We'll all be kicked out of school. They'll never let Monstacademy stay open after this," she whispered. "We've had our chance, and we've blown it." She was starting to sob loudly, and Colin tried his best to quieten her down.

"Not quite yet," Trixie whispered, distracted by something that she had seen at the entrance to an alleyway a little way along the street. She waved her hand energetically towards a water table that had been set up against the corner of the building until Colin and Gloria finally saw what she was pointing to. Leaning against the table was Heston and his two idiotic sidekicks.

Even as they watched, Heston was handing out cups of poisoned water to unsuspecting members of the public. As they walked away and took a sip, they seemed to vanish. Only Trixie and her friends knew that they were really just very small.

Whenever somebody disappeared, the people around them looked confused for a moment before apparently deciding that they must just be imagining things. Trixie and her friends started to panic.

All at once, Trixie spotted an opportunity. Heston and his friends had ducked into the newsagents and had left the bottle of potion unattended on the small trestle table that had been set up to hold the jugs of free water.

Seeing their only chance at redemption, Trixie, Gloria and Colin crept on hands and knees towards the table. Can you imagine what a sight they would have been if anybody in the crowd had bothered to turn around? A Vampire, a Werepoodle and a scruffy looking girl all crawling along the street.

Luckily, the crowd were too busy cheering

along the many colourful floats that were slowly snaking along the street to notice. Eventually, the trio of would-be heroes made it to the water table. Taking a deep breath, Trixie reached up slowly and grabbed the large glass bottle that held the clear potion.

"Quick, let's go!" she mouthed to the others. Colin shook his head.

"He'll know!" he whispered.

Trixie looked confused. What should she do? She couldn't put it back onto the table. They might not get another chance. Suddenly, Gloria smiled a wide smile that showed off her true Vampire heritage. She snatched the bottle from Trixie's hands and poured the contents into a plant pot that was home to a well-manicured olive tree. At least, it was home to what soon became a very tiny, well-manicured olive tree.

Next, Gloria reached up onto the table and pulled down one of the many jugs of water that had been intended for the crowd of people. She filled the potion bottle back to the very top with boring old water and screwed the cap back on.

Finally, she placed both the bottle and the now much emptier jug back onto the table and signalled for the other two to follow her as she fled into the crowd.

When they judged themselves to be well hidden amongst the swarm of people, they turned and watched just as Heston returned with armfuls of sweets and crisps. It appeared that he was none-the-wiser to their trick as he soon unscrewed the lid from the potion bottle and slowly added a drop into each of the water jugs.

It didn't take long before more parade goers started picking up cups of water, and Trixie and her friends were able to breathe a sigh of relief at how close they come to disaster.

As they watched, Heston moved along each of the water tables repeating his trick at each water jug. Little did he know that all he was adding to the jugs was more water!

Laughing and joking at a job well done, Trixie and her friends finally followed their head teacher's instructions and made their way back to Monstacademy.

CHAPTER 10

Another Letter

Miss Flopsbottom had decided that, as punishment for the banner fiasco, Trixie, Gloria and Colin were not allowed to attend the Halloween Dance that evening. They weren't particularly bothered. After the excitement of thwarting Heston's plan, they were looking forward to relaxing on their own and had retired to the girls' common room to relive their day's work. The subject of the banner wasn't brought up.

It was getting close to midnight, just as the party in the main hall was getting warmed up when Miss Flopsbottom entered the common room. She looked at a couple of other children who had decided to give the party a miss and who were sat reading in the corner.

"Do you mind if we talk in private?" she asked. "Let's go into the girl's bedroom for a moment. I'm sure the tidiness will be a positive influence on you Colin!" Once inside, she took a seat at the foot of Trixie's bed and invited the other two to join them.

"First," she began firmly, "I stand by my punishment for the embarrassing display with the banner today. There really was no excuse for that, and you have brought shame to the name of Monroe's Academy for the Different."

"But that was Heston!" Colin argued. "He's been spying on us all year, and I know he did that to get us into trouble. And we didn't have time to check. We were still finishing it last night!" Colin blurted before realising what he was admitting. He had the decency to look sheepish. Gloria had turned bright red and scowled.

"Be that as it may, Mr Curlyton, you had more than enough time to get it finished and I hear that you have been spending an awful lot of time in the dinner hall lately. There are no excuses." The three children hung their heads and nodded.

"However, that being said, I should not have dismissed your other accusations about Heston Gobswaddle so lightly." At this news the three heads rose swiftly and focused on their head teacher.

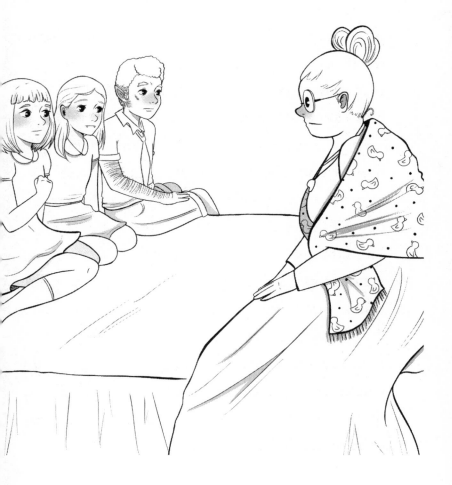

"It would appear that, acting upon an anonymous tip, our caretaker, Mr Snottington, found a bottle of shrinking potion hidden under Mr Gobswaddle's bed. Rest assured that he will be punished accordingly as soon as we can find the little blighter.

"Poor little Timothy Whipsnittle has been returned to his former size and all of the unfortunate people at the parade who had the misfortune of sampling Mr Gobswaddle's potion have all been rounded up. They will be returned to their normal size shortly and administered with a memory potion. Can you imagine if the news made it to the *Daily Ghoul*? It'd be a scandal!" Miss Flopsbottom looked worried for a moment before continuing, "I do hope that whoever found the rest of the potion that he was planning to use at the parade disposed of it carefully."

"I think you can rest assured that they did." Gloria laughed, as she was a lot quicker at understanding what Miss Flopsbottom was hinting at than the other two. "It was a tree-mendous honour." The three children broke down into a fit of giggles at Gloria's terrible joke. Miss Flopsbottom looked very confused but decided to leave well enough alone.

"Then let us speak no more of it!" Miss Flopsbottom smiled widely and headed for the door. "I will always be grateful for what you three did today. After all, you did save Monstacademy." With that, the three were left alone once again.

The rest of the term passed in a blur and soon the ground was covered in a thick layer of crisp white snow as Christmas appeared on the horizon. Trixie found that being in Miss Flopsbottom's good books didn't really mean anything to the other teachers who continued to dislike her greatly and make their lessons extra tough just for her.

Miss Brimstone was in a particularly bad mood after her snub at the Parade, and Trixie found herself sat on her own facing the wall during the Banshee's Latin lessons. She didn't mind, though. She was starting to get the hang of potions and had discovered that, when she tried, she was a natural at Snaffleball. Mr Fetch had grudgingly allowed her to play on the school team. Their first match was against Cromley's after Christmas, and Trixie couldn't have been more excited.

Soon enough the lessons wound down and it was time for the children to find their parents and go home for the Christmas holidays. It surprised Trixie to realise that she was excited to see her mum again. She hadn't heard from her all term and had a lot to tell her. She also hoped that the cats hadn't made too much of a mess of her bedroom.

But she knew that she would miss her new friends greatly. She wasn't sure how her mum would react to having a Vampire or a Werewolf over for tea, even if he was actually a Werepoodle. He'd definitely make short work of the cat circus.

Heston had been caught trying to climb out of the window during the Halloween Dance and had been suspended from the Academy. He'd been ordered to do a hundred hours of community service (picking up litter for the *freaky, ordinary* humans that he disliked so much) before he would be allowed back to Monstacademy. Trixie and her friends had vowed to keep a close eye on him after Christmas in case he decided to return to his wicked ways.

On the morning that Trixie's mum was due to pick her up, a letter arrived at the castle. Once again it was in a neat, brown envelope and stamped with the mark of Wexbridge Borough Council. It was addressed to Trixie and this time she was able to open and read it herself.

As she ripped open the envelope, her hands were shaking. The last time she'd received a letter like this it had been terrible news. Or at least it had seemed like terrible news at the time. She had no idea what it could be this time, but she knew she had to find out. With trembling fingers, she pulled the sheet of paper out of the envelope and read the letter.

She laughed out loud before balling the letter up and throwing it into the glowing embers of the fireplace.

Dear Miss Grimble,

All of us at Wexbridge Borough Council are delighted to tell you that a space has been found for you at the local comprehensive school should you still wish to leave Monroe's Academy. If you wish to take up this position, please write back as soon as possible. If not, then we trust that you will enjoy your new term.

Yours sincerely

Mr Bothwold-Oxelton

Mr Bothwold-Oxelton

P.S. Congratulations on stopping that young scalliwag's dastardly plan. As a reward I've enclosed a voucher for a year's supply of cabbage from Keith's Toilet and Vegetable Emporium on the High Street!

As the paper crackled and crumbled, she reflected that there was nowhere else she would rather be than where she was at that moment.

After all, she had a Snaffleball match to win.

Now for some
monstrously good fun!

Can you find the words that Heston has hidden in the puzzle?

```
F A P A R A D E Y I C Y
L M P Y H M O C R O M X
O X O O E N O T O E S I
P C O F S Q H L D L P R
S D D H T W E A F O I T
B E L L O E C H E E S N
O C E T N A T R I I R C
T D F E T Y R A P X A O
T G O S P A R S N I P L
O H N M J F K L B R G E
M O G L O R I A C T M N
M L N E E W O L L A H O
```

Colin   Monstacademy
Flopsbottom   Parade
Gloria   Parsnip
Halloween   Poodle
Heston   Trixie

Can you find the ten differences hidden in these pictures?

Imagine you were a monster at Monstacademy. Draw a picture of what you would look like!

The Christmas Cat Circus

The Christmas Cat Circus

'Twas the week before Christmas and all through the house not a creature was stirring. Except for the cats. The cats were on the trapeze. And the tightrope. In fact, the whole cat circus was in full swing. Trixie Grimble wasn't aware of any of this as she was trying her hardest to fall asleep. She was finding it tough because she was in the garden shed and, as I mentioned, it was very nearly Christmas and it was very, very cold.

Earlier in the year, Trixie had been sent away to boarding school after her own school had closed. It hadn't been any ordinary boarding school. Trixie had been sent away to Monroe's Academy for the Different, or Monstacademy as it was nicknamed.

Whilst she was away, Trixie's mum had wasted no time in trying to achieve what had apparently been a lifelong ambition to train a cat circus. You may have been to a circus yourself, and you may have seen the big cats performing their tricks for the audience.

This was not the type of cat circus that Trixie's mum had in mind. Those big cats simply balanced on a ball or attacked a chair held by a very brave (or very foolish) lion tamer. Grimble's Amazing Cat Cacophony was something entirely new. (Trixie's mum didn't know what cacophony meant. She just liked the way it sounded.) It had never been tried before. There was a good reason for this.

Trixie's mum had hoped to teach the dozen or so kittens that she had bought to perform the tricks normally performed by acrobats. She wanted to see them twirling on a trapeze, juggling jars of jam, tottering on a tightrope, crashing out of a cat cannon and so much more. Much to Trixie's surprise, her mum had been very successful. The cats had taken to the circus like a penguin to ice skating.

When Trixie had returned home, her mum hadn't been at home (Mr Burbage, the next-door neighbour, needed his bunions massaging and her mum was the only person who could put up with the smell) and so Trixie had made her own way up the stairs to what was once her bedroom.

The door had immediately wedged against a pile of crashmats when she tried to push it and she'd bruised her shoulder shoving it open. Inside, the room was unrecognisable. The whole of Trixie's old bedroom was filled with circus equipment from floor to ceiling. One of the cats peered at her from her old beanbag, daring her to say anything. It smelt as though the cats hadn't stopped what they were doing to take a toilet break.

"I'm very sorry. I forgot you were coming home this week, and I didn't have time to tidy it up before I collected you. You really should have called ahead to remind me!" her mum had moaned later that evening when she'd returned from the Burbage's.

"Well, where am I going to sleep? I can't sleep in there with them. It's filthy!" Trixie really wasn't impressed. How would you feel if you wandered in from school one day, threw your bag on the floor as normal and then found out that your bedroom had been taken over by a passing badger?

"I've put your old bed up in the shed for you.

You can take all of the old quilts with you. It can be like a den! You used to love playing down there."

The garden shed? Trixie couldn't believe her own mum could be so absent-minded.

"It leaks!" she'd cried.

"It's cold!" she'd wailed.

"There's probably rats!" she'd moaned.

None of it had made the blindest bit of difference. "I really am very sorry. I'll find somewhere else for the cats just as soon as I can. I can't really force them to live outside in this weather, can I? They're indoor cats."

"And what about me? I'm an indoor person! Don't I deserve to be looked after?"

"Oh, Trixie, don't be such a fusspot. This is England. It never gets that cold anyway. Besides, it's only until you go back to school."

"I'll be dead by then."

"Well, then at least the cold won't bother you. You really are very dramatic, Trixie. Is this what that Monster College has done to you?"

"It's Monstacademy, Mum, and I really don't think I'm being dramatic. I saw a polar bear on the way here. Even he had a coat on."

It had continued like this for quite some time, but, in the end, Trixie had still ended up in the shed. That first night it had snowed and it still hadn't stopped. In preparation, Trixie had stuffed a rucksack with biscuits, crisps and enough cola to last until spring.

True to her word and in a last-ditch attempt to show some sort of motherly love, her mum had helped her carry every blanket and quilt in the house down to the shed. She'd even given Trixie the one from her own bed.

Surprisingly, it wasn't as cold as Trixie had feared once she buried herself under a mountain of quilts, blankets and her dad's old coats. Trixie was able to spend the nights snuggled up warm and more comfortable than she would have been on top of a pile of cats.

Then, a few days before Christmas, a terrible thought had struck her. Santa Claus! The Big Man! Old Red Belly! No, Santa Claus wasn't the terrible thought. He's pretty nice (I've met him). But what if Santa Claus didn't know where to find Trixie? He'd spent the last nine years delivering presents to the same stocking on the same bed in the same room in the same house. What if he found her room full of cats and decided to leave them presents instead of her? She had to do something and it had to be fast.

The very next morning, Trixie set about trying to figure out what to do.

There has to be a way to let Santa know that I am in the shed, she thought.

The first job and absolutely the most essential was to fix a chimney to the shed for Santa to come down. Trixie didn't have access to a spare real chimney. Not many people do. Instead she used a large plant pot with the bottom cut out. It was a lot thinner than she expected Santa to be, but she figured he must breathe in to fit into even the most generous of chimney anyway and so he could probably fit down this.

Next, she tried to figure out a way to attract his attention. Immediately she ruled out some of the more obviously disastrous ideas like fireworks (likely to blow up his sleigh), a slingshot (unlikely to reach), yelling through a megaphone (likely to wake up Mr and Mrs Burbage next door) and a giant net strung between two lampposts (she didn't have a big enough net). There wasn't enough time to send another letter.

Then, it struck her. The perfect way to attract Santa's attention.

Trixie set about finding everything that she would need and then stepped out into the frosty morning. Her teeth started to chatter and her breath formed so much steam in front of her that she looked like a steam train making her way slowly up the garden path. When she got to the back door, she realised that she'd left her key back at the shed and so she started to throw small stones at her mum's bedroom window until she woke up and let her in.

"What are you doing, Trixie? It's far too early to be awake." Her mum looked like one of the monsters back at Monstacademy without her makeup and morning coffee.

"No time for that now, Mum. I need to borrow the cats." Trixie didn't wait to hear her mum's response and bounded up the stairs two at a time and burst into her old bedroom. The smell was overpowering, but she didn't have time to worry about that. She needed to get the cats' attention and get them started on a brand-new training regime. Her entire Christmas depended on it! Try as she might, the cats just wouldn't do as she asked. Instead, most of them just sat there licking themselves or clawing at the curtains. Trixie knew what she had to do. The cats weren't trained to do as her mum said. They were trained to do whatever the person wearing the Costume said.

The Costume was the outfit that her mum wore whenever she stepped into the circus ring and needed to put on a show. Her mum kept it stored away in a special bag in a chest in the attic. Trixie made sure that her mum was asleep before lowering the ladder and making her way into the attic and to the chest. Carefully she pulled the Costume out of the bag and hung it from one of the roof beams. The Costume was colourful and bold and garish. It was perfect for the circus. It was also a little bit too big for Trixie, but she was desperate. The trousers were scarlet red with hundreds of small white stars scattered across the legs. On her top half, Trixie wore a waistcoat made of similar fabric and a bright blue and white striped jacket. The whole hideous outfit was topped off by a blue top-hat with a single white star in the middle.

There was a full-length mirror propped against the wall and Trixie caught her reflection in it as she tried to twirl in the Costume. She looked like a walking American flag. She shuddered at how tacky she looked and reminded herself why she was doing this. The stakes were too high to give up now. Santa Claus needed to know where she was living.

This time, the cats stood to attention as soon as Trixie walked back into their bedroom. They all sat on their haunches and gave her their full attention. All she had to do now was teach them her new routine. She had planned it all in her head the night before, but it was still very difficult to get the cats to understand what she wanted them to do. This would be their finest hour. The Greatest Cat Show on Earth! It didn't help that they'd never worked with props before.

If you have a pet cat, you will know exactly how difficult it is to get them to do anything that they don't want to do. Have you ever tried to move a cat off your bed once it is comfortable? Or to get them to stop leaving you dead mice at the door?

It can't be done. Cats are the most independent and clever creatures on the planet. In fact, the only reason that they aren't running the world right now and we don't have a cat Prime Minister is because they are also the laziest creatures on the planet. A cat won't play fetch like a dog. They understand perfectly what you want them do, but they know that if they leave the ball where it is, you will fetch it for them.

You can imagine, then, just how difficult it was for Trixie to get the dozen cats that formed Grimble's Amazing Cat Cacophony to do what she wanted even when she was wearing the Costume.

Somehow, Trixie managed it just in time for Christmas Eve. She was confident that they could pull it off. Over the course of the day, she sneakily carried one cat at a time down to the shed so that they would be ready when the time came.

Each time she opened the door the cats would make a bolt for freedom until eventually she placed them all in a large cardboard box.

Trixie had also made sure that all of the circus equipment was lifted up on to the roof of the shed where it would be needed. At eight o'clock sharp, she gave her mum a kiss goodnight and headed down to the shed. She couldn't afford any mistakes, and she spent the next few hours checking that everything was ready. The sound of hammering and sawing filled the air as she set up what looked like a mini-circus ring on the flat roof of the shed.

Over the years, Trixie had worked out that Santa Claus normally visited her house just after midnight and so she forced herself to stay awake until the old clock on the wall told her there were five minutes to go. It was time for The Greatest Cat Show on Earth! Trixie was already dressed in the awful costume and used it now to get the cats to line up in their positions on the roof of the shed.

The clock in the shed struck midnight. Trixie and the cats swung into action. At her command, Simon and Steve, trapeze artists extraordinaire, started to swing back and forth towards and away from each other. Each cat held onto the trapeze with one paw whilst holding a left-over sparkler in the other. Trixie had hoped that the sparklers would form a giant X as the cats swung back and forth that she hoped would guide Santa Claus down to the shed roof. Unfortunately, a small mouse chose that exact moment to run across the shed roof and the trapeze artists all ran off into the night as they chased it into the fields behind the house.

Up above, the high-wire walkers were about to start their death-defying stunt. Trixie had woven a rope between several trees so that it formed a giant arrow pointing towards the shed. She'd chosen Richard and Rosie, the bravest of the cast, to perform this stunt and they were both wearing helmets with big wax candles on top of them. Trixie hoped that the arrow would light up as they ran across the rope.

She couldn't believe it! Both of the cats had fallen asleep on their platforms and no matter how much she shouted, they wouldn't wake up. Trixie yelled until she lost her voice. She couldn't believe it was all going wrong.

There was only one more act to go and she needed to be patient. Finally, she heard what she had been waiting for. The tiny sound of bells jingling high in the night sky. Santa was on his way and it was time for the final performance of the evening. Dennis was a big fat tomcat and was well-trained as a cat cannonball. He wore a shiny red cape and an enormous blue crash helmet. She'd lured him into the cannon earlier in the evening with a lovely fish head and all that was left for her to do was to light the fuse on the Cat Cannon. There was a loud bang and then…nothing. Dennis failed to appear. The large banner that she had painted didn't go flying into the sky. Something warm ran down Trixie's back, and she realised where the missing cat was. She grabbed a smug-looking Dennis from the branch above her head and plonked him down on the roof in front of her. He just sat there and licked his fat paws.

"You look ridiculous!" Trixie shouted in frustration. Dennis didn't care, though. Cats aren't really bothered about what they look like. Hanging from Dennis's back was the banner that Trixie had spent an hour painting. It read:

TrIxIE GriMbLe IS in tHe ShEd!!!

Trixie couldn't believe that her plan hadn't worked. After all of her planning, all of the scratched arms and scooping their poop from her wastepaper basket, it hadn't worked. There wasn't any more time now, the bells were getting louder, and Trixie knew that she had no choice but to go to bed and try to get to sleep. She slid from the roof and dived under her quilt and closed her eyes tight. She could feel her tears freezing on her cheeks.

The next morning the air was crisp and fresh. Trixie rubbed her eyes and looked around the shed sadly. Something caught her eye. Somehow, her plan had worked! The stocking that she had hung on the back of the door bulged and a thick candy cane was poking out of the top. At the foot of her bed was a pile of presents wrapped in shiny gold paper and silver ribbon. Trixie squealed and started to gather them up into an old potato sack to take up to the house.

Bright white snow exploded into the air when Trixie burst out of the shed door and into the garden. She sank into the crisp white blanket until her ankles were cold and wet, but she didn't care.

Santa had found her!

The plan had worked! She didn't know how, but it had worked! It was the first time ever that Trixie felt like something had gone right for her. Most of the cats had found their way back to the shed overnight and had been fast asleep when she woke up, but she'd made sure to leave them bowls overflowing with tuna for their breakfast.

Surprisingly, Trixie's mum was already awake and waiting at the back door to let her in with an enormous hug. Later that day, when all the presents had been opened, her mum drove her to her grandmother's where they had an enormous Christmas dinner and sang songs around a roaring fire. It was turning into a perfect Christmas for Trixie Grimble.

When they got home that evening, Trixie's mum turned to her and gave her a warm hug.

"I've got one more present for you, Trixie. I hope you like it." Her mum covered Trixie's eyes and led her up the stairs and into her old bedroom. When she pulled her hands away, Trixie was startled to see that the bedroom had been cleaned out and painted to be exactly how it was before Trixie had moved into the shed.

"What's this for?" Trixie asked.

"Well, I've been thinking. I suppose you were here first and it really is your bedroom after all."

Trixie ran and hugged her mum tightly. "Thank

you so much! I love it!"

"You know, I really thought I'd enjoy having you out from under my feet but actually, it's much nicer having you back home. Besides," her mum smiled, "the cats much prefer the garden shed!"

That night, Trixie fell asleep quickly and dreamed about returning to Monstacademy. Now that she had her old bedroom back, she wasn't quite as eager to rush back.

About The Author

Matt Beighton is a primary school teacher from the middle of England. He has two young daughters who provide a constant source of inspiration and sleepless nights.

His unfortunate classes are often the test subjects for new stories and he feels that he owes them a debt of gratitude for putting up with some of the more terrible ones over the years.

If you have enjoyed reading this book, please leave a review online. Your words really do keep me going!

To find out more visit
www.mattbeighton.co.uk

Coming Soon!

A new term means new trouble for Trixie Grimble and the rest of the Monstacademy gang.

Can Trixie win her first Snaffleball match? Can she solve an Ancient Egyptian theft? Why is Miss Flopsbottom acting so weird?

Find out in The Egyptian Treasure, arriving 2018.

To make sure you are one of the first to know all about Trixie's latest adventures, join the newsletter at http://www.mattbeighton.co.uk

Made in the USA
San Bernardino,
CA